D1299715

Who Is That?

WRITTEN BY **KATHRYN E. LEWIS**
ILLUSTRATED BY **DARCIA LABROSSE**

McGraw Hill **Macmillan McGraw-Hill**

New York   Farmington

WHO is that?

It's a *very* fat cat.

It's a dog with a hat.

4

It's a very big bat.

WHO IS THAT?

It's MOM and DAD!

8